Dear Parent:
Your child's love of reading starts here!

Every child learns to read in a different way and at his or her own speed. Some go back and forth between reading levels and read favorite books again and again. Others read through each level in order. You can help your young reader improve and become more confident by encouraging his or her own interests and abilities. From books your child reads with you to the first books he or she reads alone, there are I Can Read Books for every stage of reading:

SHARED READING
Basic language, word repetition, and whimsical illustrations, ideal for sharing with your emergent reader

BEGINNING READING
Short sentences, familiar words, and simple concepts for children eager to read on their own

READING WITH HELP
Engaging stories, longer sentences, and language play for developing readers

READING ALONE
Complex plots, challenging vocabulary, and high-interest topics for the independent reader

ADVANCED READING
Short paragraphs, chapters, and exciting themes for the perfect bridge to chapter books

I Can Read Books have introduced children to the joy of reading since 1957. Featuring award-winning authors and illustrators and a fabulous cast of beloved characters, I Can Read Books set the standard for beginning readers.

A lifetime of discovery begins with the magical words **"I Can Read!"**

Visit www.icanread.com for information
on enriching your child's reading experience.

I Can Read!™

READING
2
WITH HELP

Gilbert and the Lost Tooth

by Diane deGroat

HARPER
An Imprint of HarperCollinsPublishers

To Rachel Funk
and her brilliant students

I Can Read Book® is a trademark of HarperCollins Publishers.

Library of Congress Cataloging-in-Publication Data is available.
ISBN 978-0-06-125214-3 (trade bdg.) — ISBN 978-0-06-125216-7 (pbk.)

12 13 14 15 16   SCP   10 9 8 7 6 5 4 3 2 1   ❖   First Edition

Contents

Chapter 1: The Wiggles

Gilbert had a loose tooth.

It wiggled during spelling.

It wobbled when he walked.

And it hurt when he bit into

his sandwich.

"Maybe it will fall out today,"

Patty said.

"Don't forget to put it

under your pillow if it does."

Patty smiled.

She had a big window in her mouth.

Frank and Margaret had windows too.

Lewis didn't have a window
in his mouth.

Lewis didn't even have a loose tooth.

He didn't want to hear about teeth.

He wanted to play kickball.

"Gilbert!" Lewis shouted.

"It's your turn.

Stop playing with your tooth

and kick the ball!"

Gilbert kicked, but he missed

and fell on his bottom!

"Uh-oh!" he said, holding his mouth.

"My tooth came out!"

Patty said, "Yay, Gilbert!

Now the tooth fairy will come."

Lewis didn't say, "Yay!"

He said, "Gilbert, stop playing

with your tooth and kick the ball!"

Gilbert put the tooth into his pocket.

Then he kicked the ball

and made a run.

Everyone said, "Yay!"

Except Lewis.

When the bell rang,

Lewis picked up the kickball.

He picked up the soccer ball.

He picked up the baseball.

And he picked up something

small and white.

After school, Gilbert ran home.

"My tooth fell out!" he shouted.

"Let me see it," Lola said.

Gilbert reached into his pocket.

But he didn't find a tooth.

He found a hole!

Gilbert ran to Mother and cried,

"I lost my tooth!"

Mother smiled and said,

"It's about time, Gilbert.

It was very loose."

"No," Gilbert said.

"I mean I REALLY lost my tooth.

I can't find it!

I can't put it under my pillow!"

Mother said, "Hmmm . . .

Maybe you can leave

a note for the Tooth Fairy

to tell her what happened."

"I'm going to leave a note too,"
Lola said.

"Maybe the Tooth Fairy
will bring me something."

"But you didn't lose a tooth,"
Gilbert said.

"She doesn't know that," Lola said.

Gilbert wrote a note.

Dear Tooth Fairy,
I lost my tooth today.
I mean I <u>Really</u> lost it.
Can you leave something
under my pillow anyway?
I will be more careful next time.
Thank you.
Your friend,
Gilbert

XXX

Lola wrote a note too.

That night, Gilbert put the note
under his pillow.

Lola put her note under her pillow.

And Lewis put a small white tooth
under his pillow.

Chapter 3: The Wake-up

When the sun went down
and the moon came up,
the Tooth Fairy went to work.
She packed her bag full of gifts
and money.
She turned on her magic tooth-detector
and flew into the night.
She flew over the rooftops
until her tooth-detector lit up.
When she was right over Lewis's house,
it grew brighter and brighter!
"I found one!" she said.

She crept into Lewis's room and
peeked under his pillow.
She found a small white tooth.
"My tooth-detector is always right!"
she said.
But before she put the tooth
into her bag, she looked at it closely.

Then she looked at Lewis snoring

with his mouth open.

"Hmmm . . . ," she said.

Suddenly the tooth-detector buzzed

and beeped like crazy.

It was pointing toward Gilbert's house!

The next morning, Gilbert looked
under his pillow and found money!
Mother said, "The Tooth Fairy
must have seen your note, Gilbert."
Gilbert put the money
into his piggy bank.

Lola looked under her pillow.

She found a pink toothbrush.

Mother said, "The Tooth Fairy

must want you to take care

of your teeth, Lola."

Lola brushed her teeth very hard.

Maybe they would come loose!

Lewis looked under his pillow.

He didn't find money.

He didn't find a toothbrush.

He found a note that said:

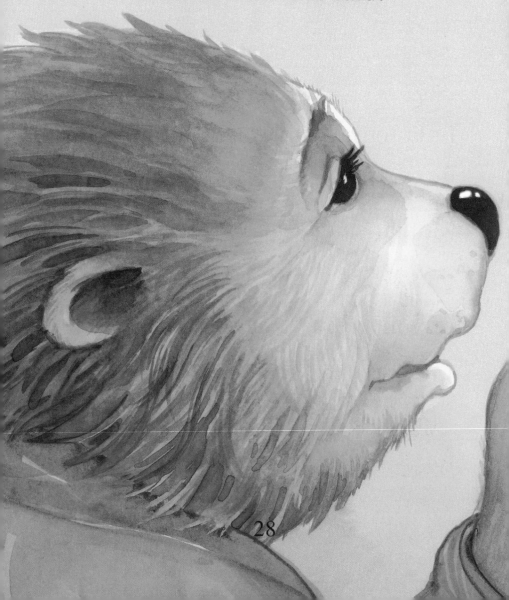

Dear Lewis,

I found a tooth under your pillow, but I do not think it is yours. Sometimes my tooth-detector can be wrong!

I will be back again when you REALLY lose a tooth.

Your friend,

The Tooth Fairy

"Oops," Lewis said.

At recess, Gilbert told everyone
about the note he had left
under his pillow.

Lewis wondered if he should tell
everyone about the tooth
he had found on the playground.
He wondered so hard that he
didn't see the ball coming.
It hit him right in the face!

"OW!" Lewis cried.

But then he felt something

wiggly and wobbly in his mouth.

"My tooth is loose!" he shouted.

Everyone said, "Yay!"

Even Lewis.